Chloe the Clumsy Cheetah

BY D.J. MOSS

ILLUSTRATION FLOR ITZEL ESCOBAR

For Raymond & Macsen Love Dad

First published in 2022 on Kindle Direct Publishing

ISBN: 978-1-7396713-0-3

Chloe the Clumsy Cheetah

BY D.J. MOSS

ILLUSTRATION FLOR ITZEL ESCOBAR

Chloe the cheetah was ever so fast,
she waved at her friends as she ran straight past.

Past lion, past tiger, past ostrich, past hyena,
so fast past tortoise that he barely did see her.

But speedy Chloe could never win a race,
she's always falling flat on her face.

Her paws were so quick they would get in a muddle, she'd end up face first down in a puddle.

As she'd lie there all muddy and feeling glum,
past they'd all go shouting "keep up chum!"

Even Tony the tortoise would say,
"you'll never win a race running that way!"

Her friends would all clap as she was last over the line,
"chin up Chloe you'll have better luck next time."

But she thought to herself "it's not to do with luck,"
she's tripped over everything, from crocodile to duck!

**The next day she called a rematch around the lake,
but Chloe made a bet you just should not make.**

**If they could beat her, she'd bring them their dinner,
but Chloe knew that she'd be the winner.**

Everyone across the zoo had come to join in,
they all knew that Clumsy Chloe couldn't win.

She set off so quickly, she thought today was her day,
slowing down just slightly, so on her feet she could stay.

Chloe pictured everything that had made her fall,
a tree stump, a warthog, even an acorn so small!

While she was looking for things that
had tripped her before, in the trees ahead,
there was such an uproar!

AH
AH
AH

The mischievous monkey was at it again,
he thought of himself as the zoo's comedian.

His plot for today was to slow down the cheetah,
so all her friends surely would beat her.

Chloe's mind was still focused on all the times she'd tripped,
as the monkey threw a banana he laughed as she slipped.

While she lay in a heap, she knew another win she'd missed,
but at least she could add banana skin to her tripping list!

FINISH

Late that night, after gathering everyone's food,
Chloe was lying down in a terrible mood.

When along came the wise old wildebeest to say,
"not to worry, you'll win one day."

Chloe cried "What's the point of being the fastest if I never win?"
He replied "Look at how happy you've made all your friends
and let that sink in! "

"You could win every race by a country mile,
but isn't it more important that you've made all your friends smile?
Don't concentrate on when you've lost in the past,
we all know that you're extremely fast!
Today you've brought everyone their dinner,
and in our eyes that makes you the real winner!"

I have a lot more friends!
Marcus the Mischievous Monkey,
Harry the Handsome Hippo,
Raymond the Raging Rhino and
Gary the Greedy Gorilla.
Would you like to meet them?
Look out for the other Zoophoria Safari Park stories!

Printed in Poland
by Amazon Fulfillment
Poland Sp. z o.o., Wrocław